Ian Falconer

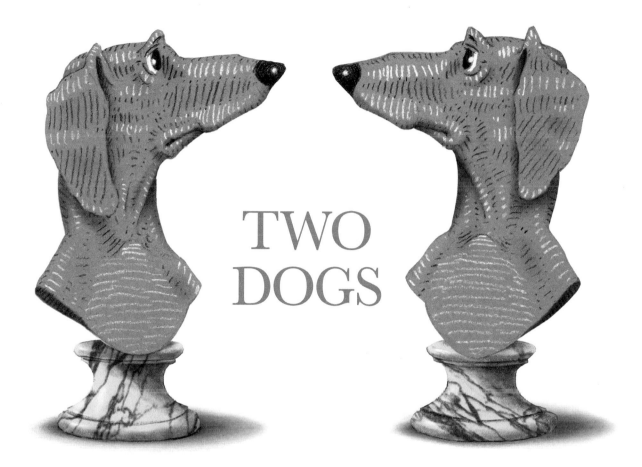

TWO
DOGS

Two dogs, dachshunds.
Dignified, slightly imperious,
with aquiline noses and noble profiles.
Indeed, they look like little Roman emperors.

MICHAEL DI CAPUA BOOKS ¤ HARPER COLLINS PUBLISHERS

Except when they look like this.

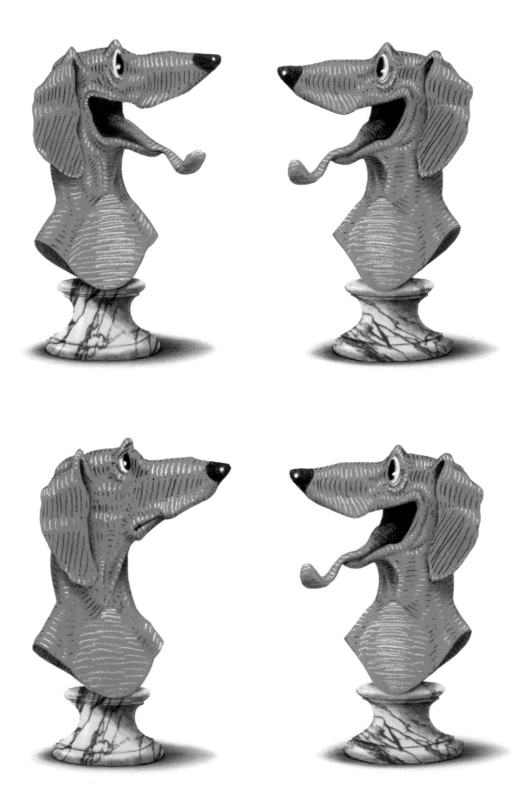

Most of the time Augie looked more serious.
Perry was all over the place.

When they were puppies,
everyone loved Augie and Perry—
and played with them all the time.

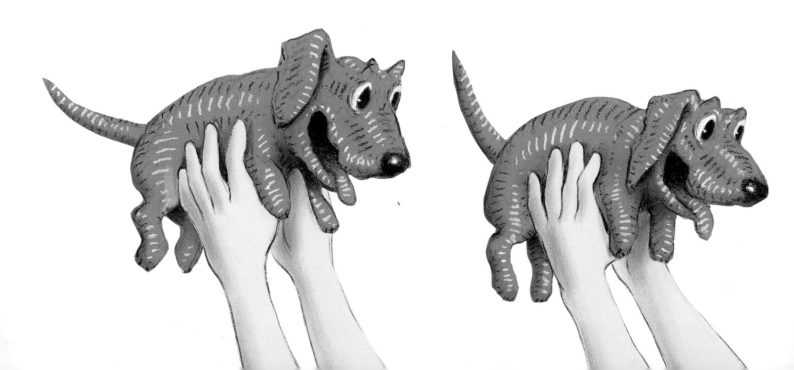

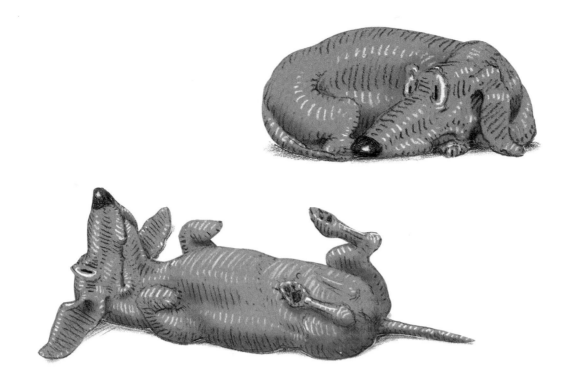

But over the years the children had gone off
to school. The parents were at work.

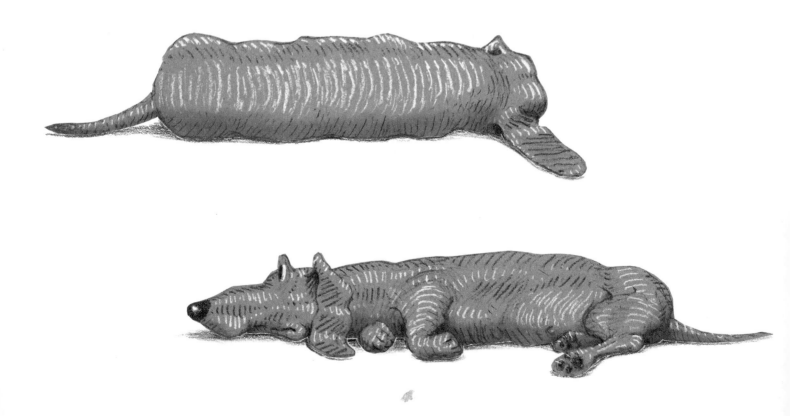

And like so many other dogs, they were left alone.
All day. Most days.

They were bored.

Much of the time they spent barking at squirrels in the backyard.

Sometimes Perry would steal Augie's ball.

The ball was very important to Augie.

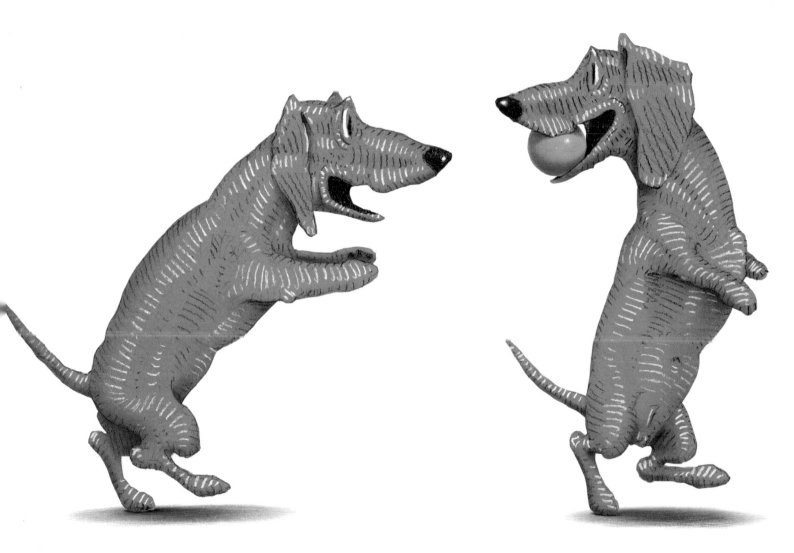

"Please, Perry, give me back my ball!"

"Perry, please give
me back my ball!"

"GIVE ME BACK MY BALL!"

"No."

"Fine."

"Augie, where are you going?"

"PLEASE, AUGIE, NO!
NOT THE PIANO!"

Perry howled in agony.

Finally, Perry returned the ball.

"We can't go on fighting like this.
We have to escape."

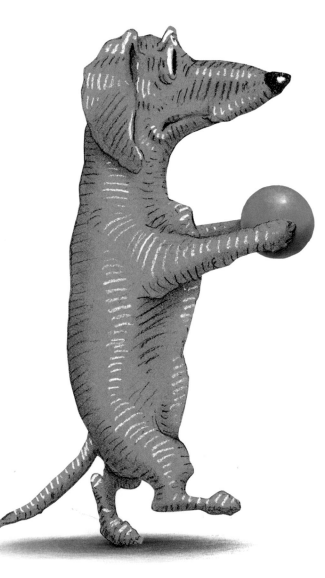
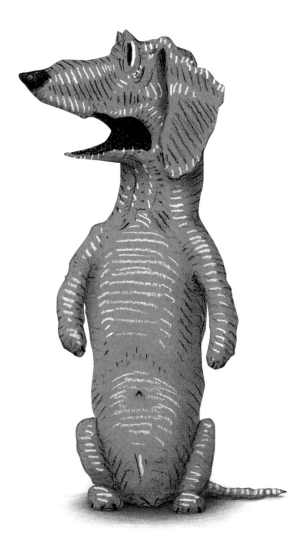

Perry started barking
at the lock.

That didn't work.

woof!
woof!

"Stop jumping, Perry. I'll do it."

Augie neatly flipped the lock.

First thing they did was water the mother's new flowers.

They found some raccoon poop
and happily rolled around in it.

They loved the swings.

And the seesaw.

Then Perry wanted to go swimming.
Augie wasn't at all sure about this.

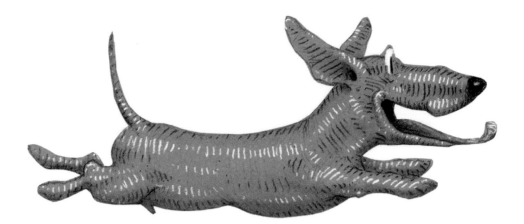

Perry just went for it . . .

BELLY FLOP!

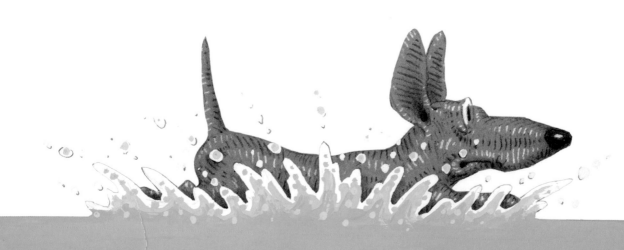

Augie nailed it.

"Look, Augie!
A hole!
It might be a mouse,
it might be a mole!"

"But we can't
dig up the lawn,"
said Augie.
"WE'LL GET
IN TROUBLE!"

"But
we'll get
to dig!!"

Dachshunds love to dig,
and in the end even Augie couldn't resist.

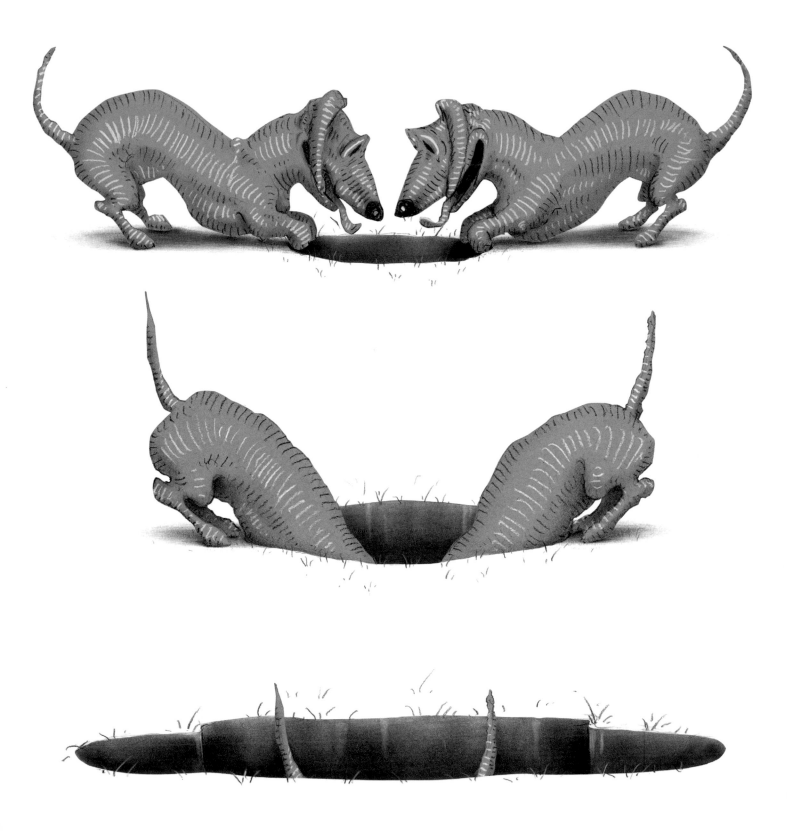

Then
they
heard
the
car
drive
up.

They hightailed it back to the house.

Now *Perry* was the one who was worried.
"We're going to get in TROUBLE, Augie!"

"NO WE'RE NOT. Just do what I do.
Hurl yourself at the door and bark!"

"Oh my goodness!" the mother shrieked.
"WHAT HAPPENED!
Who on earth dug that hole?"

"A SQUIRREL!
It was HUGE!"

"HUGE!" echoed Perry.

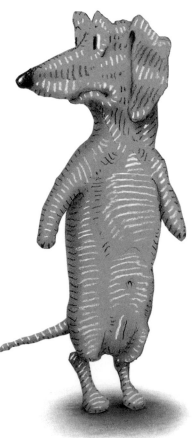

"...HUGE,
with BIG FANGS,
and GIANT CLAWS and—"

"Enough, Perry.
Now you're just
humiliating yourself."

It didn't matter, really, because
the mother never learned to speak Dog.

"Oh, my little angels," the mother cooed.

"You deserve
an extra treat tonight!"

They had the mother fooled.

And although sometimes they still disagreed . . .

"Once again, Augie,
 I saved the day."

"No, you didn't."

At least they were, for the most part, friends again.

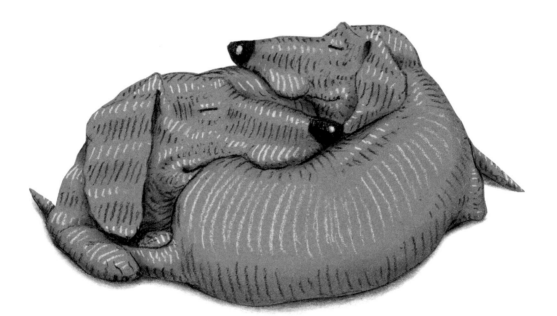

Text and pictures copyright © 2022 by Ian Falconer

Library of Congress Control Number: 2022930513

HarperCollins Publishers, New York, NY 10007

Printed and bound by Phoenix Color

Art digitally adjusted by Rick Farley

Book design by Ann Bobco

First edition, 2022

22 23 24 25 26 PC 6 5 4 3 2 1